ARNOLD
THE
SUPER-ISH HERO

HEATHER TEKAVEC & GUILLAUME PERREAULT

KIDS CAN PRESS

Arnold worked in the family superhero business, but he wasn't exactly a superhero.

He wasn't super strong like his cousin Marvella, able to lift a fire truck with just one finger.

He wasn't super fast like his brother Rocket, able to fly across the city at lightning speed.

BOING

He wasn't super bouncy like his uncle Flip, able to leap off tall buildings and land without a single scratch.

Actually, Arnold was just the phone guy.

But he *was* able to take important messages with really neat printing.

Neato!

Everyone expected Arnold's superpower to show up any day. His parents were retired superheroes. His grandparents were, too. Even his great-grandmother on his father's side had been a superhero.

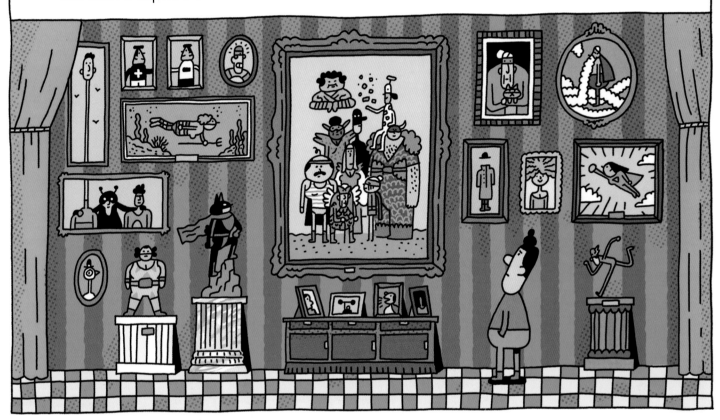

Every day, the others would ask ...

Have you found your superpower yet?

It was no use. All Arnold could do well was answer the phones, and that definitely wasn't a superpower. It was more of an average office skill, really.

One mostly peaceful day, Arnold answered a call.

I need a superhero in City Park right away!

We're on our way!

He rang the alarm ...

but nobody came.

All the superheroes were already out saving the world. Or possibly eating donuts in the park.

"I must do something!" Arnold said in his best superhero voice, which squeaked a little. He read the family motto on the wall:

STOP THE BAD GUY
FROM BEING A BAD GUY

He was sure he could do that. He dusted off his great-grandmother's mask and cape and left Superhero HQ.

"I'm off!" Arnold proclaimed as he filed onto the city bus in an orderly manner.

He couldn't fly like Rocket would have ...

but when the bus stopped, Arnold leaped off super fast and ...

OOPS

almost cleared the sidewalk puddle.

Now, he had to find the crime.

Down the street, Arnold saw a man yelling at an old lady in a wheelchair.

He ran over.

You have yelled at this lady for the *last* time!

Marvella would have hurled the man into a recycling bin.

Arnold wasn't that strong, so he poked him really hard instead.

"My grandmother lost her hearing aid," the man said. "I'm just telling her to keep her hands off the wheels so I can push."

Arnold thought for a second.

Then he spotted a stray kitten.

When he put it in the lady's lap, she took her hands off the wheels and wrapped them around the kitten.

But Arnold still had a job to do.

On the bridge, he noticed a girl throwing things into the pond.
Littering was a crime! Arnold ran over and declared ...
You have littered for the *last* time!

The girl looked up. "I'm just feeding the ducks," she said, then added sadly, "but they aren't sharing with the baby duck."

Arnold took a handful of seeds and shimmied cautiously under the bridge. Uncle Flip would have leaped off the side, but Arnold was a little afraid of heights.

When he got to the water, he hand-fed the littlest one.

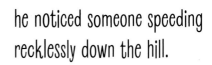

Thank you!

Looking again for the mysterious crime ...

he noticed someone speeding recklessly down the hill.

Oh, sure, anytime.

As the skateboarder left, Arnold noticed a girl crying in the sandbox. She jumped up when she saw him.

You came!

Arnold recognized the little voice from the phone. Sniffling, the girl held out a note. "I got a message to meet my friend by the nice clean sand, but she didn't come. She must be lost. You have to find her!"

"May I see?" Arnold asked. If there was one thing that he was an expert on, it was messages.

He had written down hundreds.

With super neat printing.

He examined the note.

Aha! This note doesn't say 'nice clean sand.' It says, 'ice-cream stand'!

Arnold and the girl ran to the corner, where they could see the ice-cream stand and a girl waiting there with two cones.

Arnold beamed as he wandered through the park.

He couldn't find any villains, but he did tie a few shoelaces ...

and pull a kite out of a tree before leaving.

Back at Superhero HQ, all the superheroes were crowded around the
TV watching a news flash: "Secret hero helps the good guys!"

Arnold blushed and tucked the cape and mask into his back pocket. When the others turned and saw him, he looked just like Arnold, the phone guy.

Hey, Arnold, find your superpower yet?

Well ... I'm pretty good at keeping secrets.

Everyone smiled. "Keep trying," they said and went back to work. And so did Arnold.

But sometimes, he still answered phones.

To Justin, a super son-in-law, and my super grandson, Theodore — H.T.

Published in Canada and the U.S. by Kids Can Press Ltd.

25 Dockside Drive, Toronto, ON M5A 0B5

Kids Can Press is a Corus Entertainment Inc. company

www.kidscanpress.com

The artwork in this book was rendered in Photoshop.
The text is set in Revla Sans and Boudoir.

Edited by Kathleen Keenan
Designed by Michael Reis

Printed and bound in Shenzhen, China, in 10/2020 by Imago

CM 21 0 9 8 7 6 5 4 3 2 1

Library and Archives Canada Cataloguing in Publication

Title: Arnold the super-ish hero / Heather Tekavec & Guillaume Perreault.
Names: Tekavec, Heather, 1969- author. | Perreault, Guillaume, 1985- illustrator.
Identifiers: Canadiana 20200304429 | ISBN 9781525303098 (hardcover)
Classification: LCC PS8589.E373 A76 2021 | DDC C813/.6—dc23

Kids Can Press gratefully acknowledges that the land on which our office is located is the traditional territory of many nations, including the Mississaugas of the Credit, the Anishnabeg, the Chippewa, the Haudenosaunee and the Wendat peoples, and is now home to many diverse First Nations, Inuit and Métis peoples.

We thank the Government of Ontario, through Ontario Creates; the Ontario Arts Council; the Canada Council for the Arts; and the Government of Canada for supporting our publishing activity.